SUN UP

for my grandson, Loren Tresselt Fulton   A. T.

for my daughters, Mathilde and Alexandra   H. S.

Text copyright © 1949, 1991 by Alvin Tresselt
Illustrations copyright © 1991 by Henri Sorensen

First Edition 1 2 3 4 5 6 7 8 9 10

Library of Congress Cataloging in Publication Data
Tresselt, Alvin R. Sun up / by Alvin Tresselt ; illustrated by Henri Sorensen.
p.   cm. Summary: Follows the activities of a farmer and his son from sunrise to sunset on a hot summer day.   ISBN 0-688-08656-X. — ISBN 0-688-08657-8 (lib. bdg.) [1. Farm life—Fiction. 2. Thunderstorms—Fiction. 3. Summer—Fiction.] I. Sorensen, Henri, ill. II. Title. PZ7.T732Su   1991 [E]—dc20
90-35144 CIP AC

ALVIN TRESSELT

SUN UP

ILLUSTRATED BY HENRI SORENSEN

Early in the morning, before the sun rose,
when the first birds sang,
even while everyone was asleep,
the rooster flapped his wings and crowed,
Cock-a-doodle-doo!

Another day was beginning.
Slowly the sky in the east grew light,
waiting for the sun to appear.
One by one the stars faded out,
till only the morning star glowed
in the brightening sky.

Bit by bit the sun inched up above the edge of the land,
and the purple night shadows slipped away
to sleep in dark corners.
The sun spied on a tiny field mouse as she scurried about,
looking for breakfast.
The sun sparkled on the dewdrops
hanging in a spider's web.

The sun shone on a farmer and his helper
on their way to the barn to milk the cows.
And the sun peeked in the window
at the little boy asleep in bed.
Wake up!

The sun climbed higher in the sky,
and the day grew hotter.
Now the morning mists were gone,
and tall sunflowers creaked on their thick stalks
to face the sun.

The farmer squinted his eyes
at the bright sun overhead.
"Today will be a scorcher," he said to his helper.
He started up the tractor and pulled the hay baler
out to the hayfield.

The little boy felt the heat of the sun
on his back as he walked through the meadow
with his dog.
He heard the crickets chirp and rasp
in the tall, fragrant grass.
And a catbird scolded at him
from a blackberry patch.
Now the day was very hot, and everything
hid from the burning sun.

Lazy cows lay in the shade of a sycamore tree.
They chewed their cud
and flicked flies with their thick ropy tails.
The chickens scratched and clucked,
taking dust baths in the shadow of the barn.

The little boy went into the shadowy woods to fish,
but even the sunfish hid in the cool blackness
at the bottom of the pond.

Only the farmer and his helper were about.
Round and round the field went the hay baler
—*gunka ka CHUNG, gunka ka CHUNG, gunka ka CHUNG*—
gathering the sweet-smelling hay into neat bales.

But the sun shone on in the cloudless blue sky,
and nobody could remember when there had been such a hot day.
Then suddenly, everywhere and at the same time,
everything was still.
The crickets stopped chirping.
The catbird ended his song and cocked his head.
The cows swallowed their cud and rolled their eyes.
The farmer stopped the noisy tractor
and mopped his head with a large red bandanna.

And the little boy ran out of the woods
and looked up into the hazy sky.
From the distance came a low rumble of thunder,
and everyone heard it at once.
And the muttering thunder rolled over the sky.
Slowly at first, then faster and faster,
angry black clouds boiled up to hide the sun,
and jagged lightning forked through the clouds.

A hot wind stirred the dust in the barnyard,
and the trees turned pale as the wind
twisted back their leaves.
The little boy joined his father and the helper,
and they quickly ran back to the barn.

The wind blew harder, and the trees tossed.
On rolled the thunder, and ripe drops of rain
came plopping down.
The chickens squawked and scooted back to the henhouse.
The cows crowded one another as they squeezed
through the barn door.

And the dog hid away under the farmhouse porch.
The little boy stood close beside his father
and watched the slashing rain beat down on the
muddy ground.
He saw the lightning leap across the sky.
He felt the mighty thunder shake the barn.
And he could smell the wet freshness of the summer rain.

But at last the wind grew still.
The thunder rolled farther and farther away,
over the stormy sky.

The rain turned to a drizzle, and the sun shone once more
through torn pieces of clouds.
Birds sang gayly in the rain-washed coolness,
and a delicate rainbow arched across the sky.

The clouds turned pink and scarlet
as the sun sank down in the west.
In the deepening blue of the sky
hung the new moon, with a single bright star
sparkling beside it.

The farmer and his helper got ready to milk the cows again.
The boy whistled for his dog
and went in to wash for supper.

Once more the purple night shadows woke up
and stole quietly out of the corners.
And the rooster settled himself on his perch,
tucked his head under his wing, and went to sleep.